Start with
Words and Pictures

Words and ideas by
Shirley Burridge

Pictures by
Katy Sleight

Oxford University Press

Oxford University Press
Walton Street, Oxford OX2 6DP

Oxford   New York   Toronto   Madrid
Delhi   Bombay   Calcutta   Madras   Karachi
Kuala Lumpur   Singapore   Hong Kong   Tokyo
Nairobi   Dar es Salaam   Cape Town
Melbourne   Auckland

and associated companies in
Berlin   Ibadan

Oxford and *Oxford English* are trade marks
of Oxford University Press

ISBN 0 19 431200 3 (Paperback)
© Oxford University Press 1985

First published 1985
Second edition 1986
Sixth impression 1992

Set in Helvetica Medium and Black (infant characters) by
Tradespools Limited, Frome, Somerset.
Cover photograph by Pictor
Printed in Hong Kong

Aa

a

a cup
a = 1

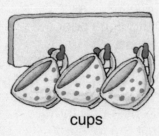

cups

above

Ann

Peter

Ann is **above** Peter

Peter is below Ann

across

across the road

along the road

add

$$5 \atop {+ \; 2} \over 7$$

add 2
add = +

$$5 \atop {- \; 2} \over 3$$

subtract 2

2

address

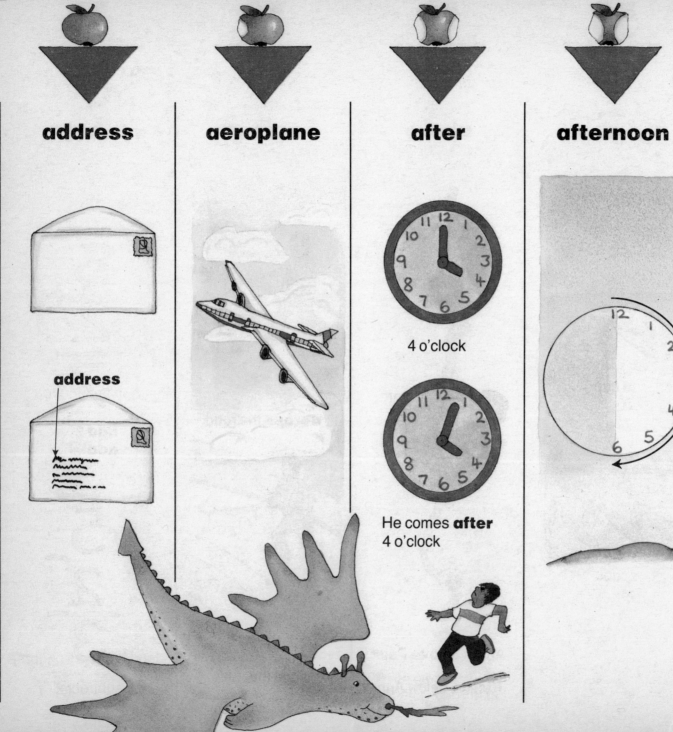

address

aeroplane

after

4 o'clock

He comes **after**
4 o'clock

afternoon

again

Peter falls

Peter falls **again**

. . . and **again**

ago   airport   all   along   also

Bob Smith — now

Some leaves are on the ground

across the road

Ann is unhappy

Bob Smith —
50 years **ago**

All the leaves are on the ground

along the road

Jane is **also** unhappy

Bob Smith —
70 years **ago**

| **an** | **and** | **angry** | **animals** | **ankle** |

an apple
an = 1

David

apples

David **and** Jean

and = +

John is **angry**

animal

animal

animal

animal

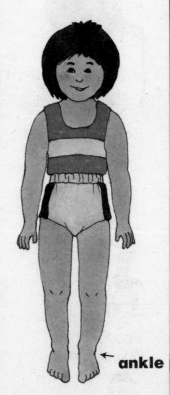

← **ankle**

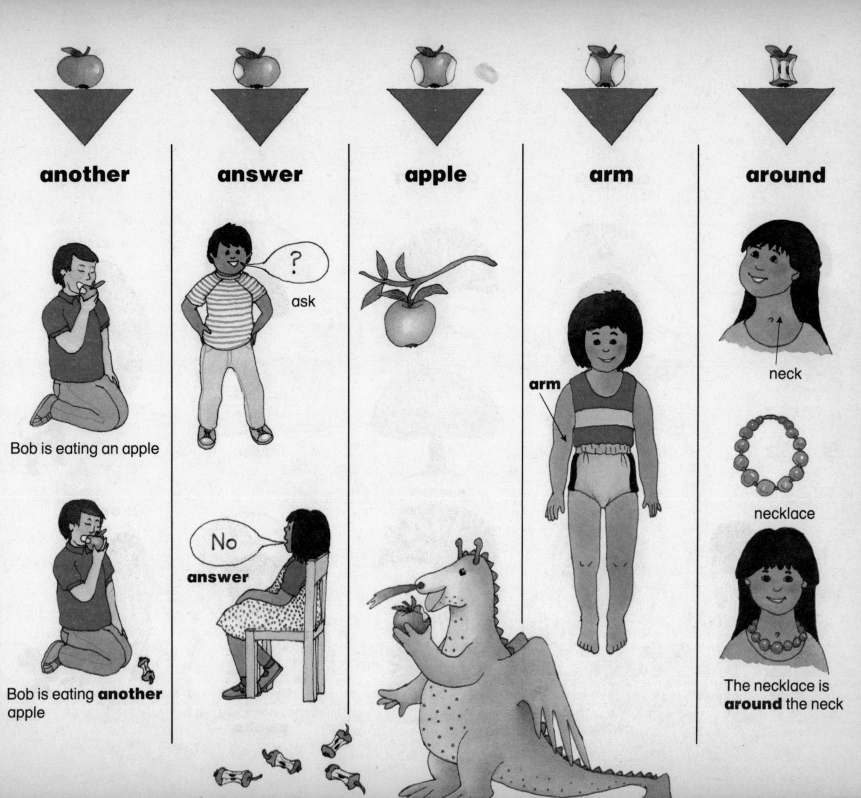

another

answer

apple

arm

around

Bob is eating an apple

Bob is eating **another** apple

ask

No

answer

arm

neck

necklace

The necklace is **around** the neck

6

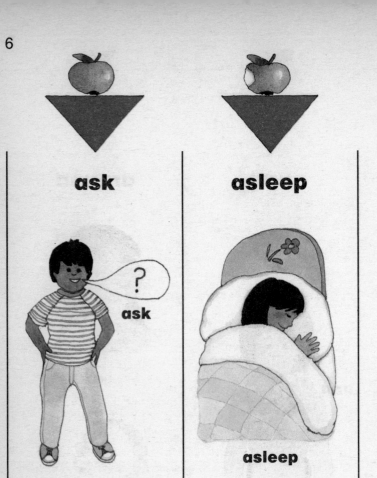

ask

ask

No

answer

asleep

asleep

awake

autumn

spring

summer

autumn

winter

awake

asleep

awake

away

'Come here'

'Go **away**'

B b

baby

back

Ben is at the **back** of the class

Ben is at the front of the class

bag

bag

bag

baker

baker

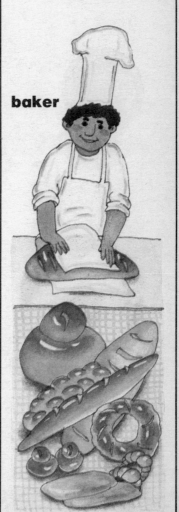

8

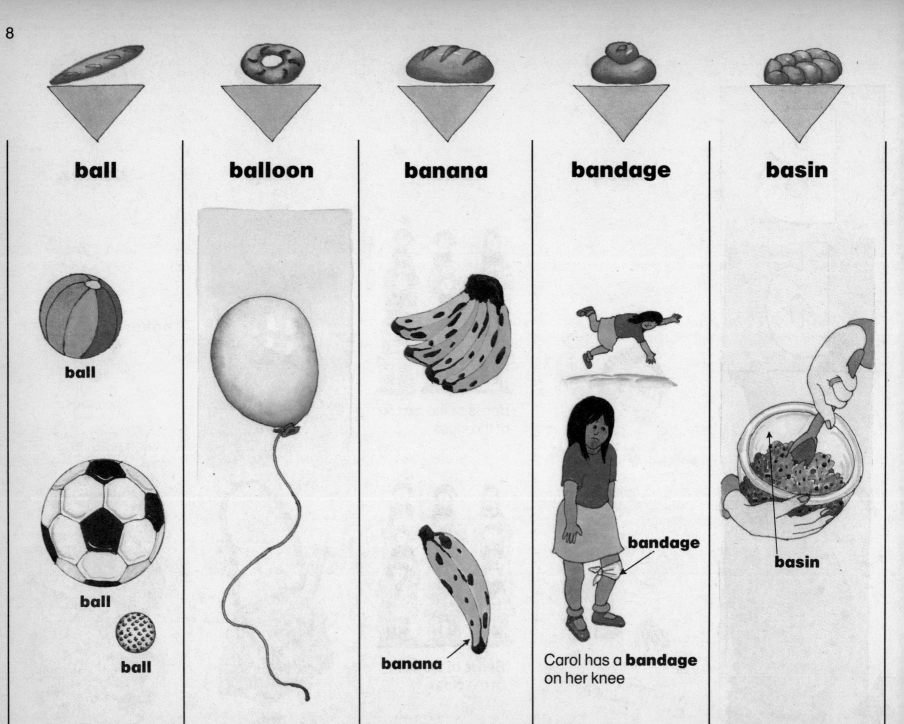

ball

balloon

banana

bandage

basin

ball

ball

ball

banana

bandage

Carol has a **bandage** on her knee

basin

9

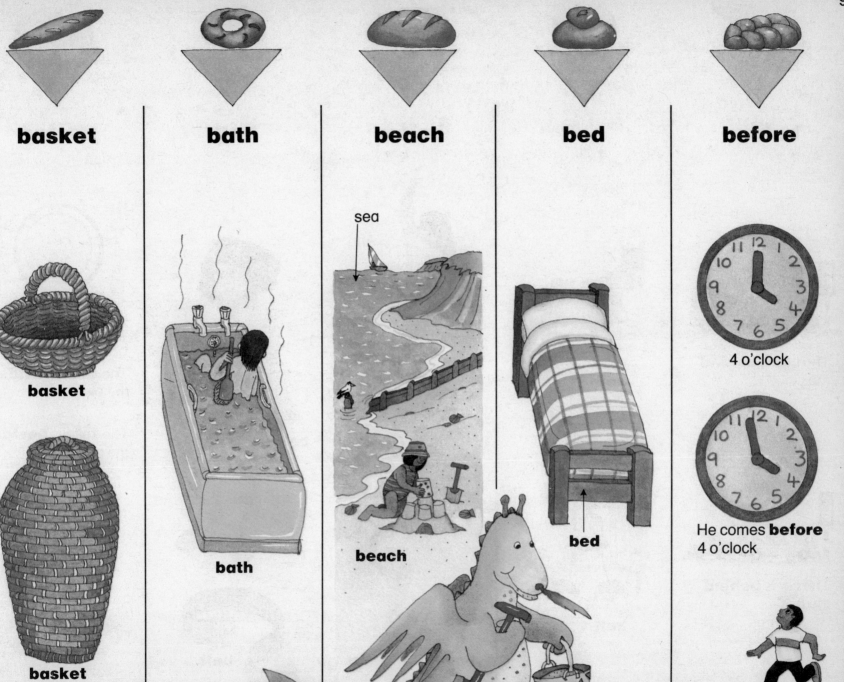

basket

bath

beach

bed

before

basket

bath

sea

beach

bed

4 o'clock

He comes **before** 4 o'clock

basket

10

| **behind** | **bell** | **below** | **belt** | **beside** |

car   bus

The bus is **behind** the car

The car is **behind** the bus

bell

bell

Ann

Peter

Ann is above Peter

Peter is **below** Ann

belt

belt

fork   plate   knife

The fork is **beside** the plate

The knife is **beside** the plate

| **bicycle** | **big** | **bird** | **biscuit** | **black** |

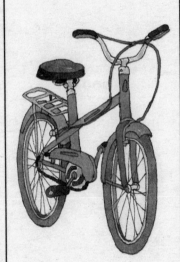

a **big** dog

bird

bird

a small dog

biscuit

Ann is eating
a **biscuit**

bird

12

 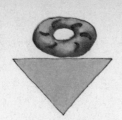   

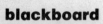

blackboard   blanket   blue   boat   book

blackboard

blanket

blanket

boat

boat

boat

book

book

book

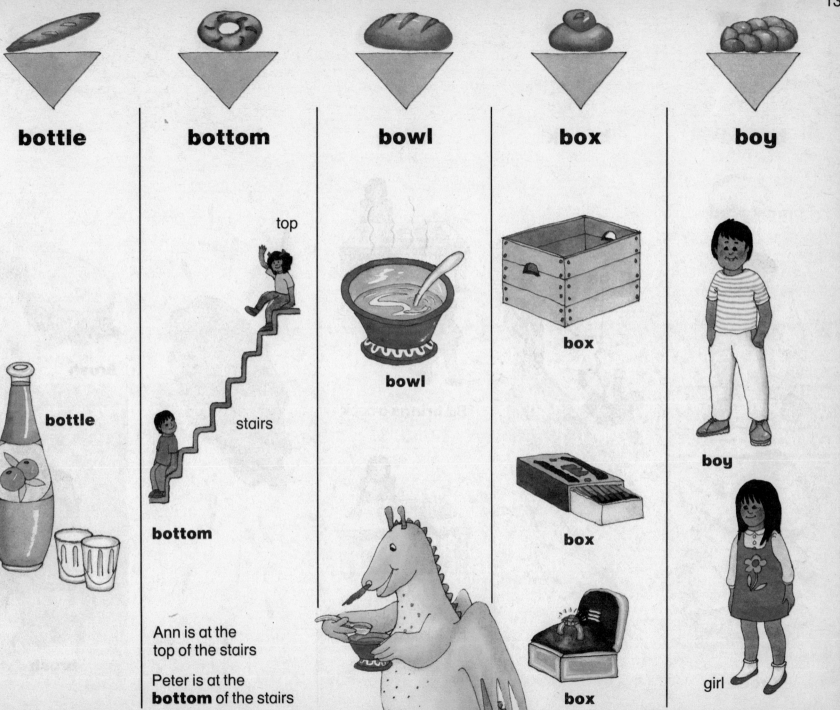

13

bottle

bottom

bowl

box

boy

bottle

top

stairs

bottom

Ann is at the
top of the stairs

Peter is at the
bottom of the stairs

bowl

bowl

box

box

box

boy

boy

girl

14

bread

break

bring

brown

brush

bread

break

Bill **brings** a book

Bill takes a book
away

brush

brush

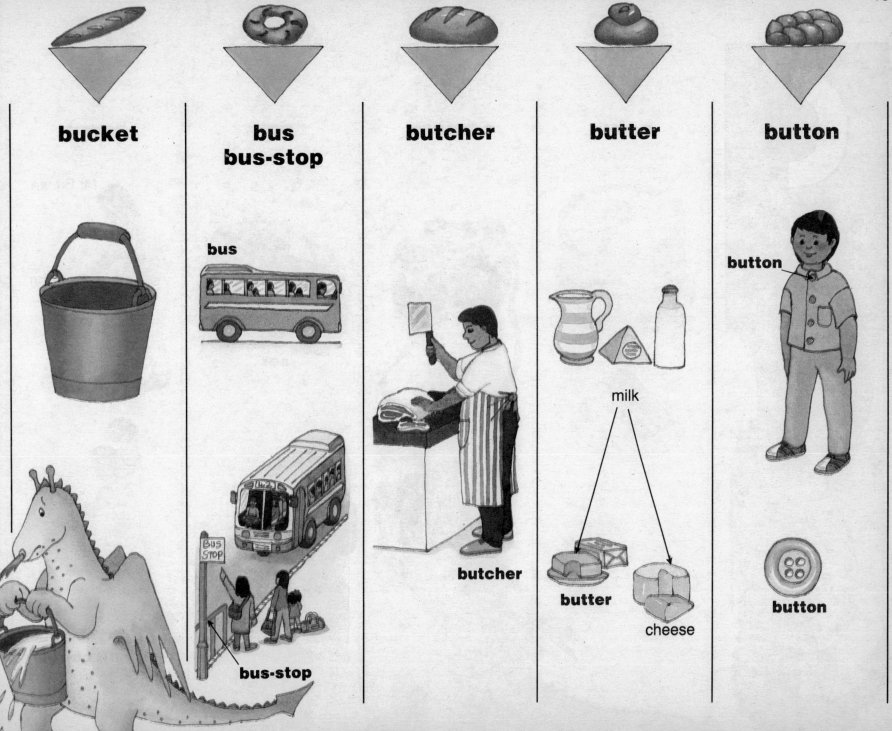

bucket

bus
bus-stop

butcher

butter

button

bus

bus-stop

butcher

milk

butter

cheese

button

button

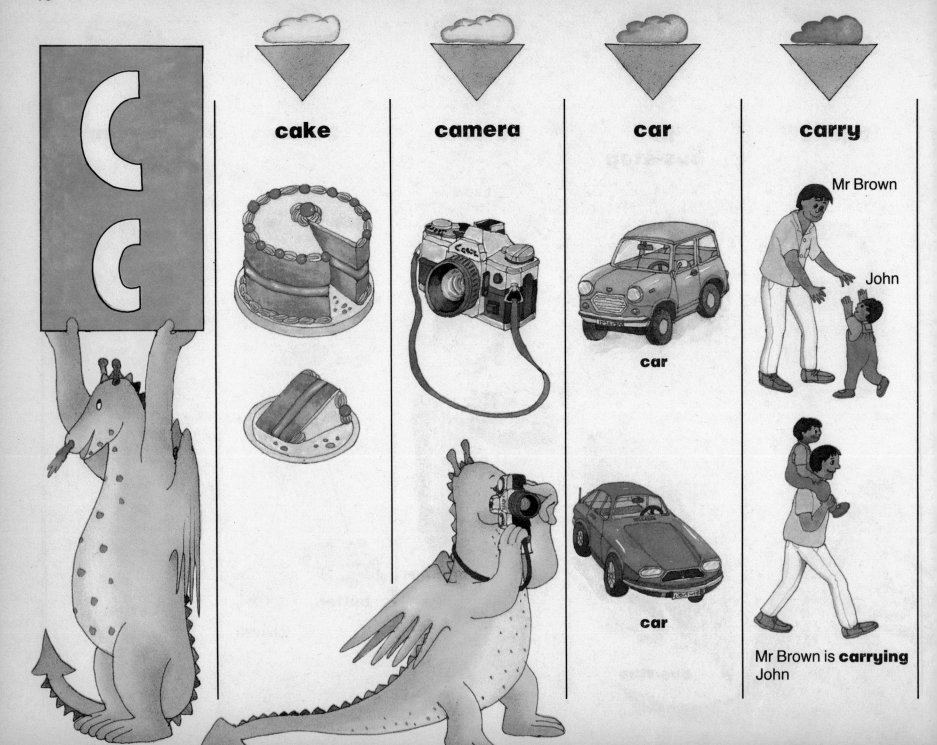

cake

camera

car

carry

Mr Brown

John

car

car

Mr Brown is **carrying** John

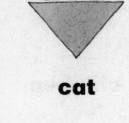

cassette

cat

catch

ceiling

chain

cassette

cat

throw

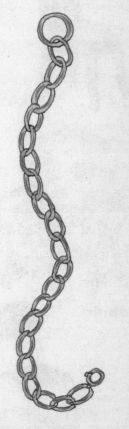

ceiling

floor

kitten

catch

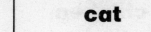

chair

chalk

cheese

chicken

child

chair

chair

chair

chalk

chalk

milk

butter

cheese

chicken

chicken

child   **child**

chocolate	church	circle	clap	class classroom

chocolate

chocolate

chocolate

church

church

church

circle

circle

square

clap

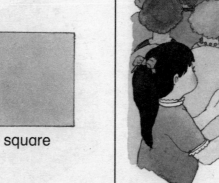

clap

class classroom

class

classroom

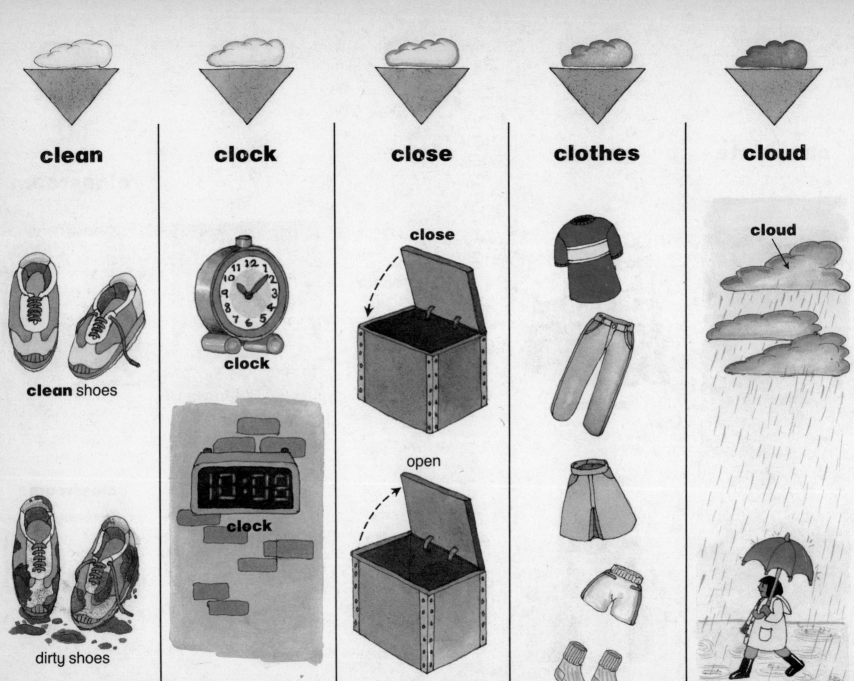

clean

clock

close

clothes

cloud

clean shoes

dirty shoes

clock

clock

close

open

cloud

coat　　**cold**　　**collar**　　**comb**　　**come**

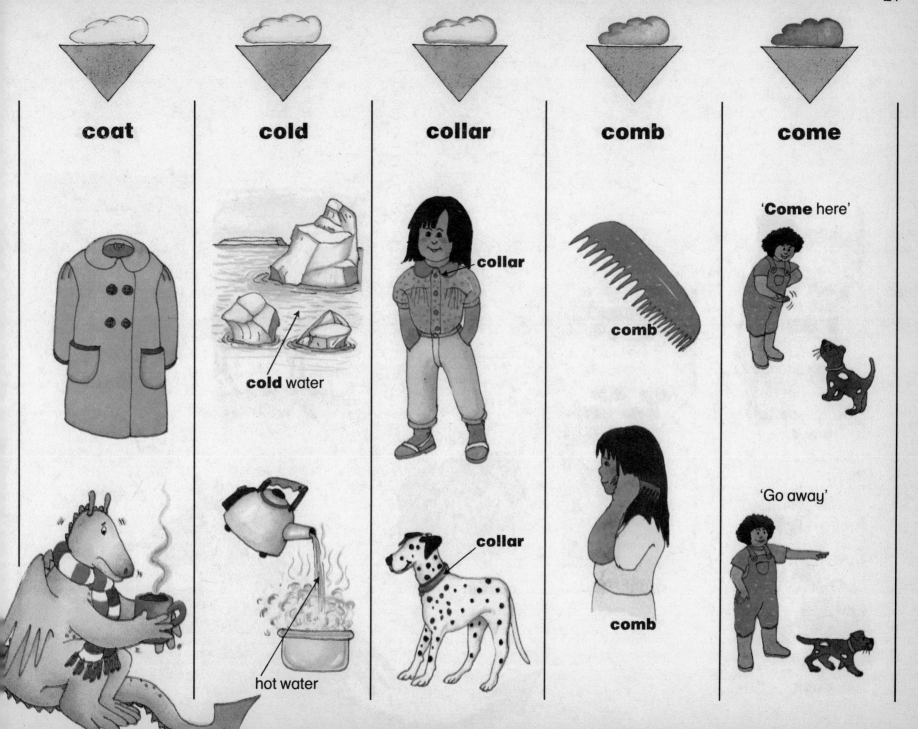

cold water

hot water

collar

collar

comb

comb

'**Come** here'

'Go away'

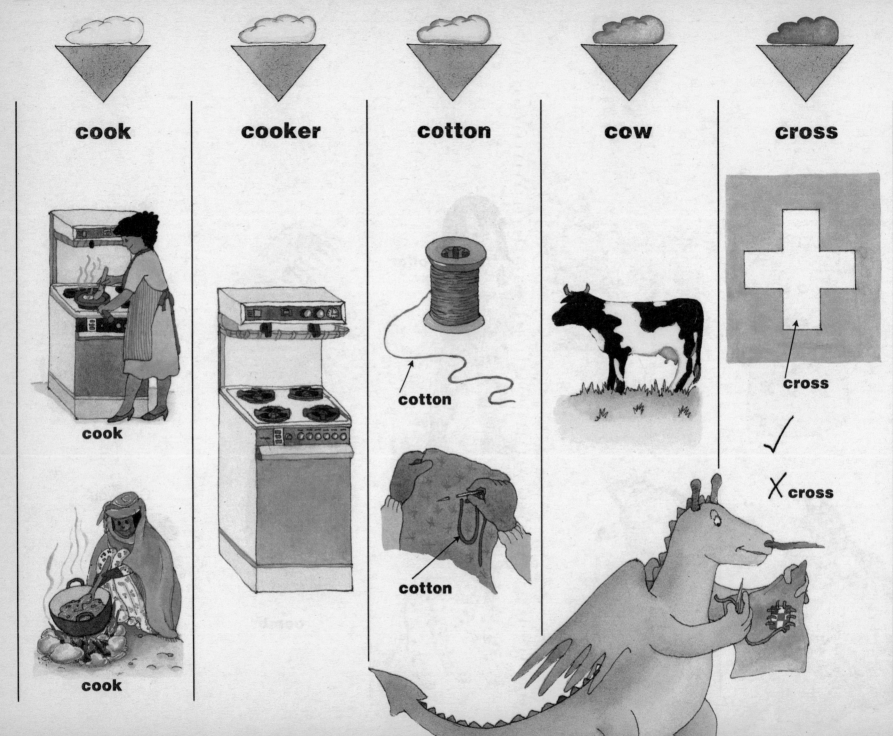

cook

cooker

cotton

cow

cross

cook

cook

cotton

cotton

cross

✓ cross

✗ cross

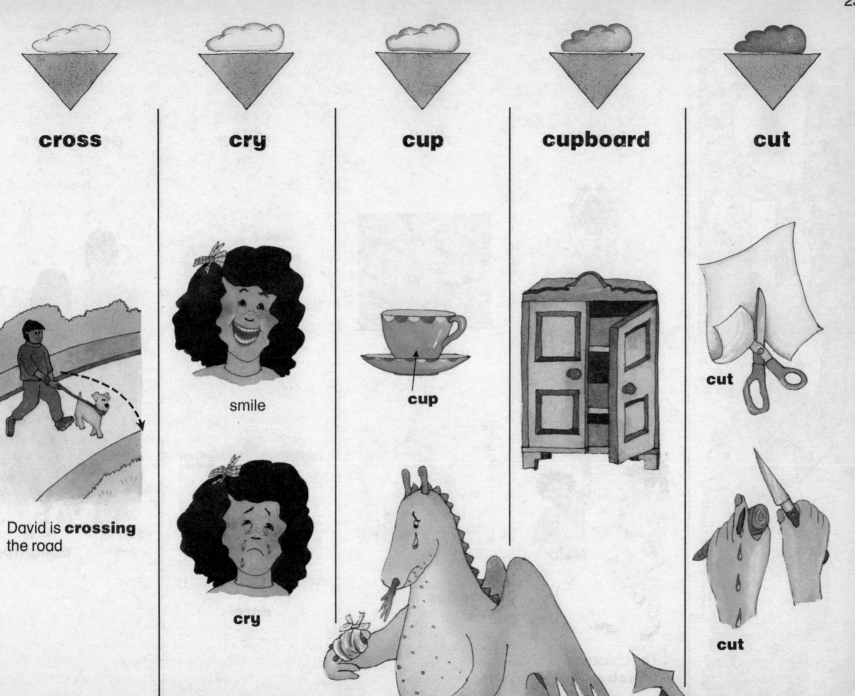

cross

cry

cup

cupboard

cut

David is **crossing** the road

smile

cry

cup

cut

cut

D d

dance

Mimi is **dancing**

The children are **dancing**

dark

a **dark** room

a light room

date

date

SEPTEMBER

SUN		7	14	21	28
MON	1	8	15	22	29
TUES	2	9	16	23	30
WED	3	10	17	24	
THURS	4	11	18	25	
FRI	5	12	19	26	
SAT	6	13	20	27	

date

daughter

son

daughter

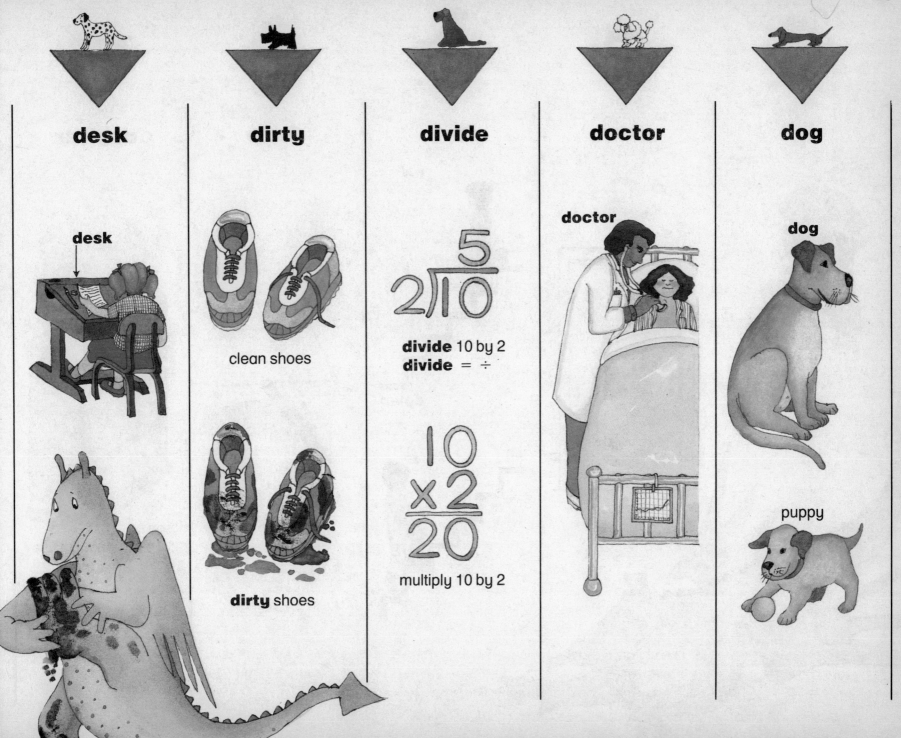

desk

desk

dirty

clean shoes

dirty shoes

divide

divide 10 by 2
divide = ÷

$$10 \times 2 = 20$$

multiply 10 by 2

doctor

doctor

dog

dog

puppy

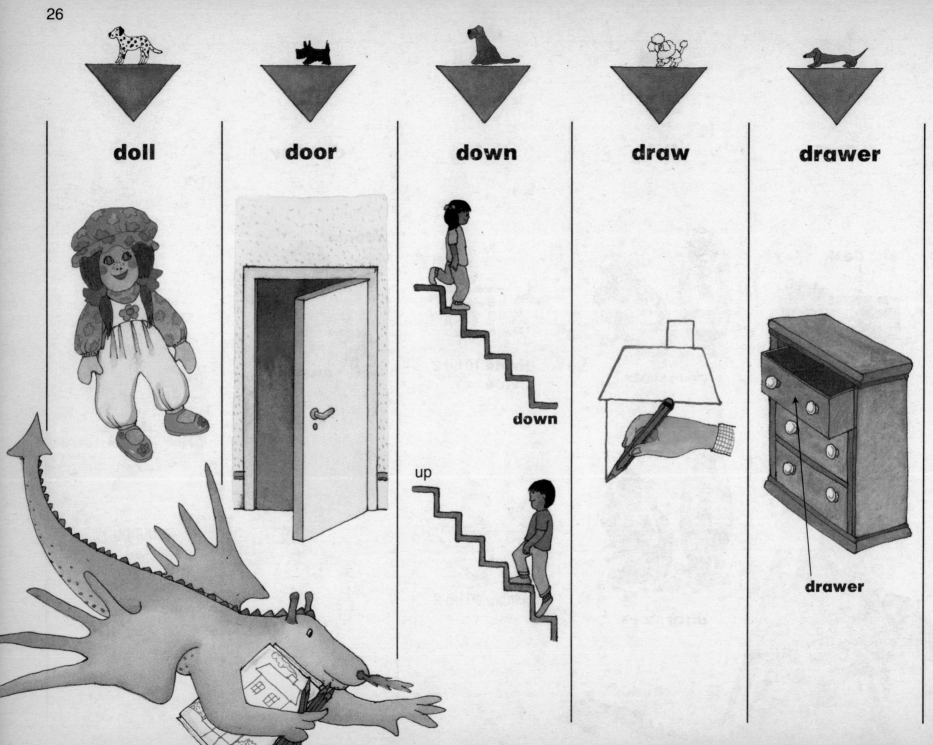

doll

door

down

down

up

draw

drawer

drawer

dress

drink

driver

drum

duck

drink

drink

driver

drum

drum

E e

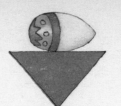

ear

ear

ear

eat

eat

eat

egg

egg

egg

eight
eighteen
eighty

eight = 8

eighteen = 18

eighty = 80

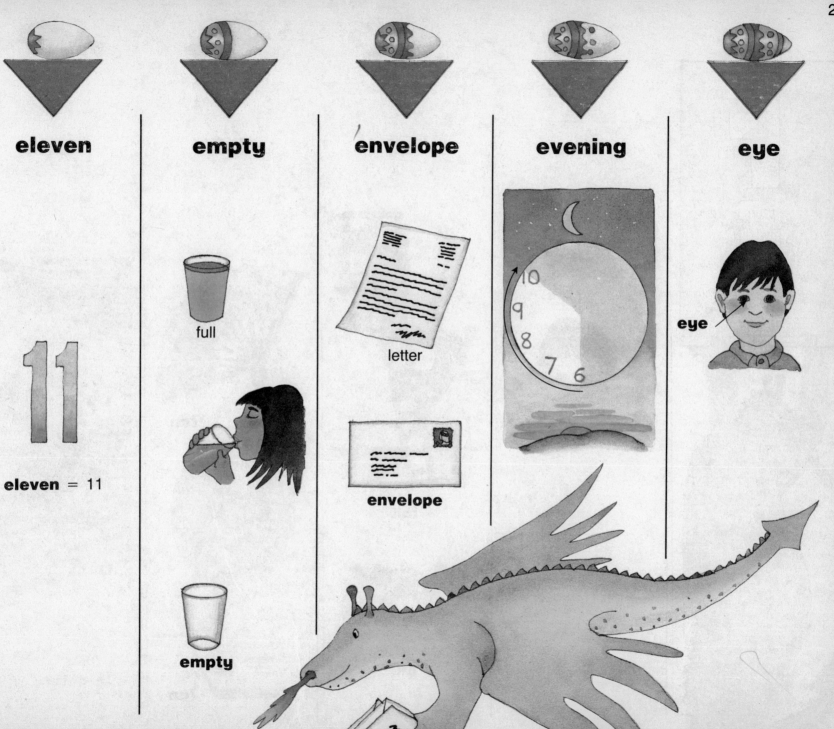

eleven

empty

envelope

evening

eye

11

eleven = 11

full

letter

empty

envelope

eye

F f

face

fall

fan

farm

face

fall

fall

fan

fan

fast

fat

father

feet

fence

1 km in 5 hours
= slow

1 km in 5 minutes
= **fast**

Fred is **fat**

Tim is thin

father

mother

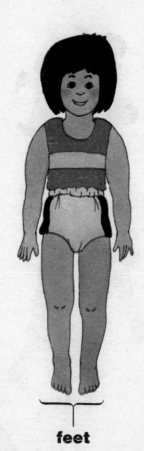

feet

fence

fifteen	**fight**	**finger**	**fire**	**fireman**
fifty				**fire-engine**

fifteen = 15

fifty = 50

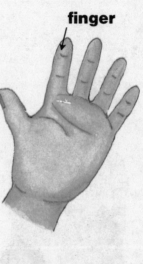

fight

fight

finger

finger

fire

fire

fire

fire-engine

fireman

| **first** | **fish** | **fisherman** | **five** | **flag** |

first
second   third

first / 1st May

first   last

fish

fish

fish

5

five = 5

floor

flower

fly

fly

food

ceiling

floor

flower

flower

flower

fly

fly

foot

football

fork

forty

four
fourteen

foot

spoon

football

fork   knife

football

forty = 40

four = 4

fourteen = 14

fridge **frog** **front** **fruit** **full**

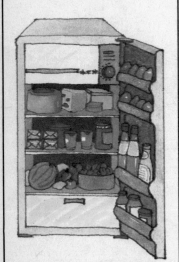

Ben is at the back
of the class

Ben is at the **front**
of the class

full

empty

This bottle is **full**
of water

37

Gg

gate

girl

give

glass

gate

boy

girl

give take

a **glass**

a window

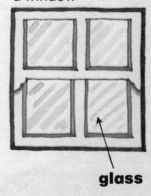

glass

glasses

go

goal

goat

grass

'Come here'

'**Go** away'

goal

grass

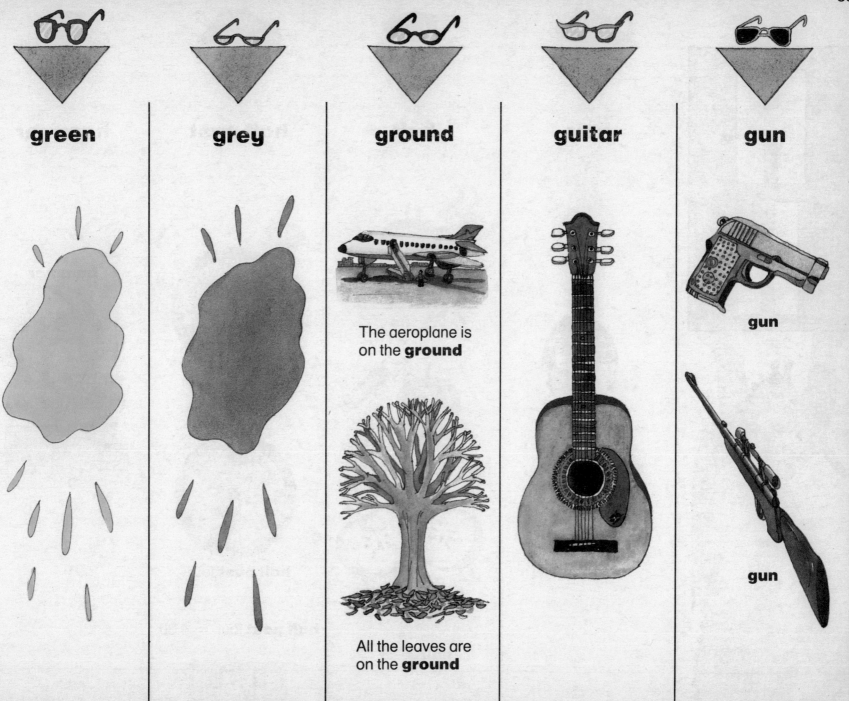

green

grey

ground

The aeroplane is
on the **ground**

All the leaves are
on the **ground**

guitar

gun

gun

gun

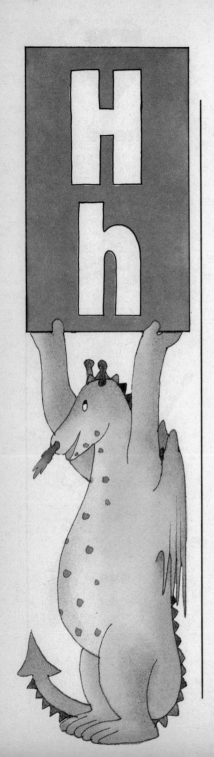

hair

hair

half

half   half

half = ½

half past

four o'clock

half past four

half past four = 4.30

hammer

hammer

hand   **handkerchief**   **happy**   **hat**   **head**

hand

handkerchief

handkerchief

Jim is **happy**

Jim is sad

hat

head

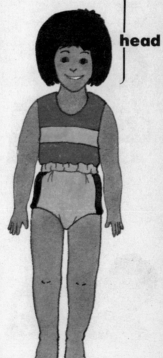

42

hear

heavy

heavy · light

The baby is light

Mother is **heavy**

hear

hear

hen

here

Here is the car

There is the car

hole

hole

hole

horse　　**hot**　　**hour**　　**house**　　**hundred**

cold water

1 **hour**

1 **hour** = 60 minutes

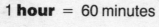

hot water

hundred = 100

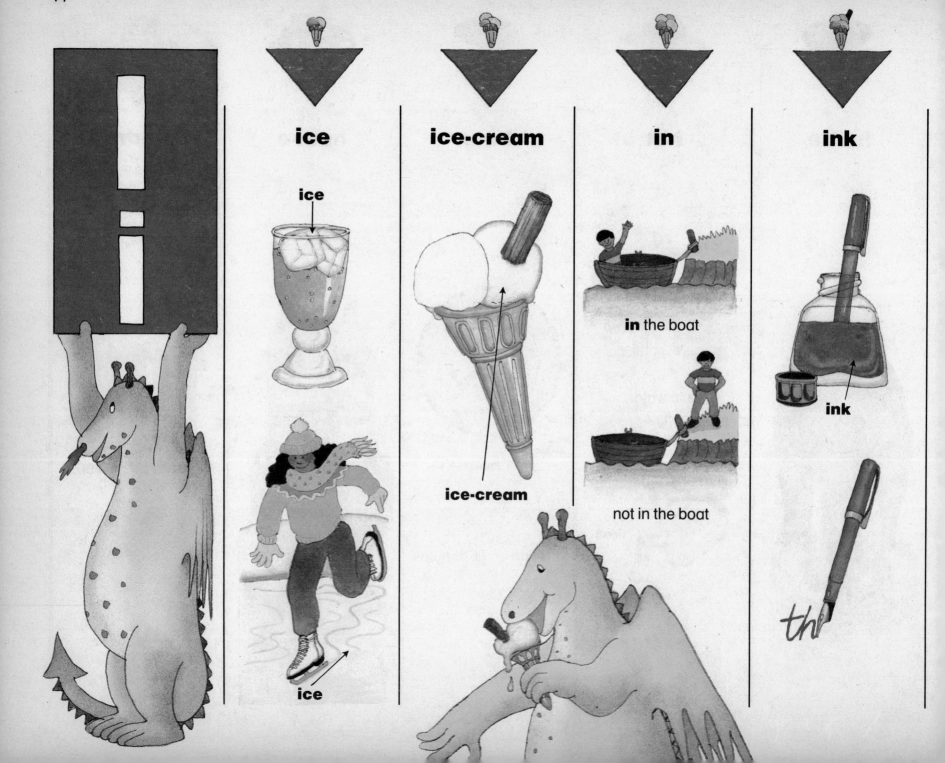

I i

ice

ice

ice

ice-cream

ice-cream

in

in the boat

not in the boat

ink

ink

th

J j

jacket

jeans

jug

jump

jacket

jacket

jeans

jug

jug

walk

run

jump

key **kick** **king** **kite**

key

king

key

kick

queen

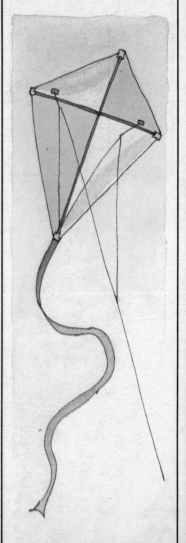

kitten	knee	kneel	knife	knock

 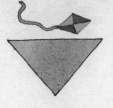   

kitten

cat

kitten

knee

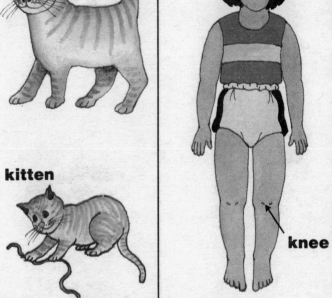

knee

kneel

stand

sit

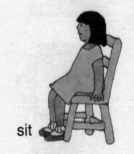

kneel

knife

spoon

fork   knife

knife

knives

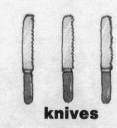

knock

knock

48

L l

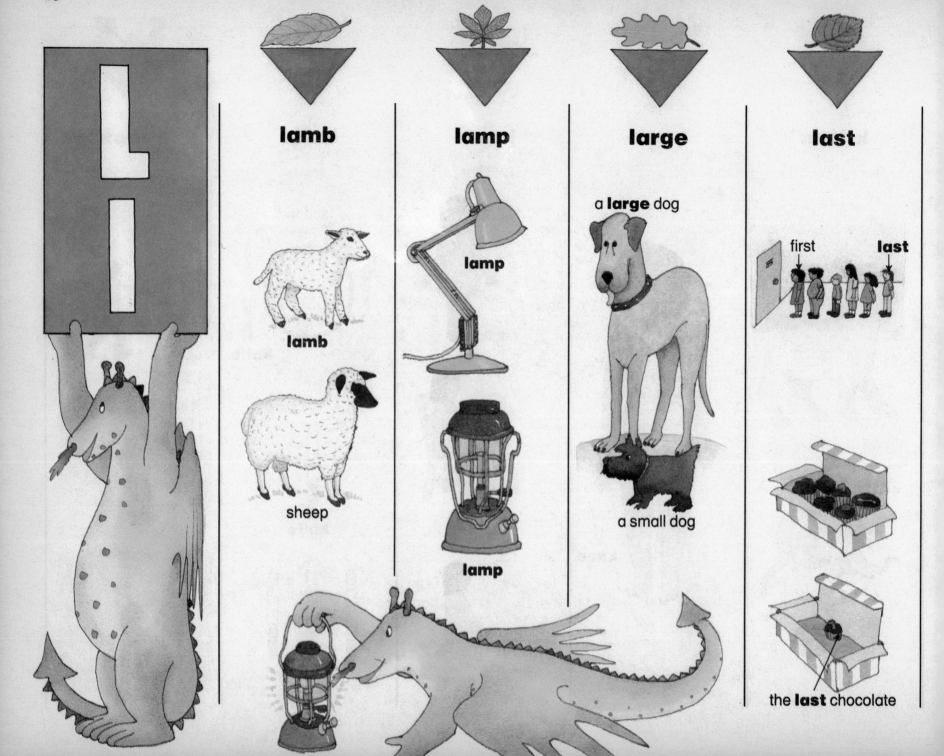

lamb

lamb

sheep

lamp

lamp

lamp

large

a **large** dog

a small dog

last

first   last

the **last** chocolate

laugh

leaf

left

leg

lemon

leaf

smile

laugh

leaves

right
hand

left
hand

left
hand

right
hand

leg

leg

letter

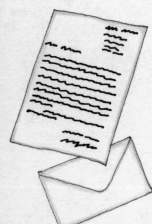

light

a dark room

a **light** room

light

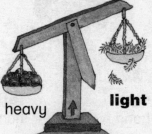

heavy   **light**

The baby is **light**

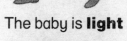

Mother is heavy

light

light

light

light →

line

circle

square

line

a **line** of trees

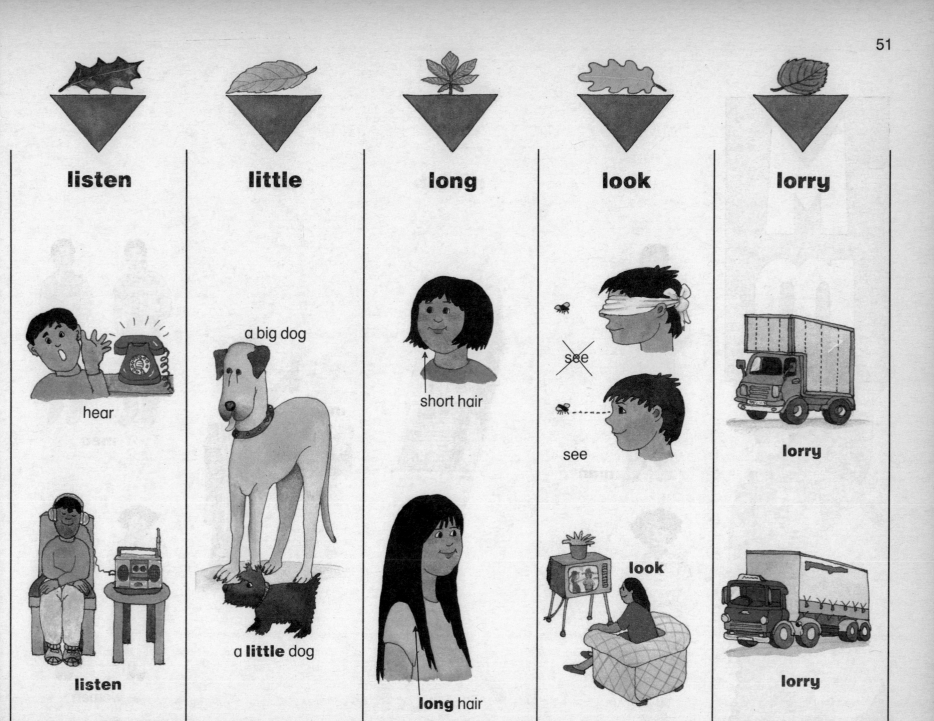

listen | **little** | **long** | **look** | **lorry**

hear

listen

a big dog

a **little** dog

short hair

long hair

see

see

look

lorry

lorry

man

match

meat

men

man

meat

men

woman

match

women

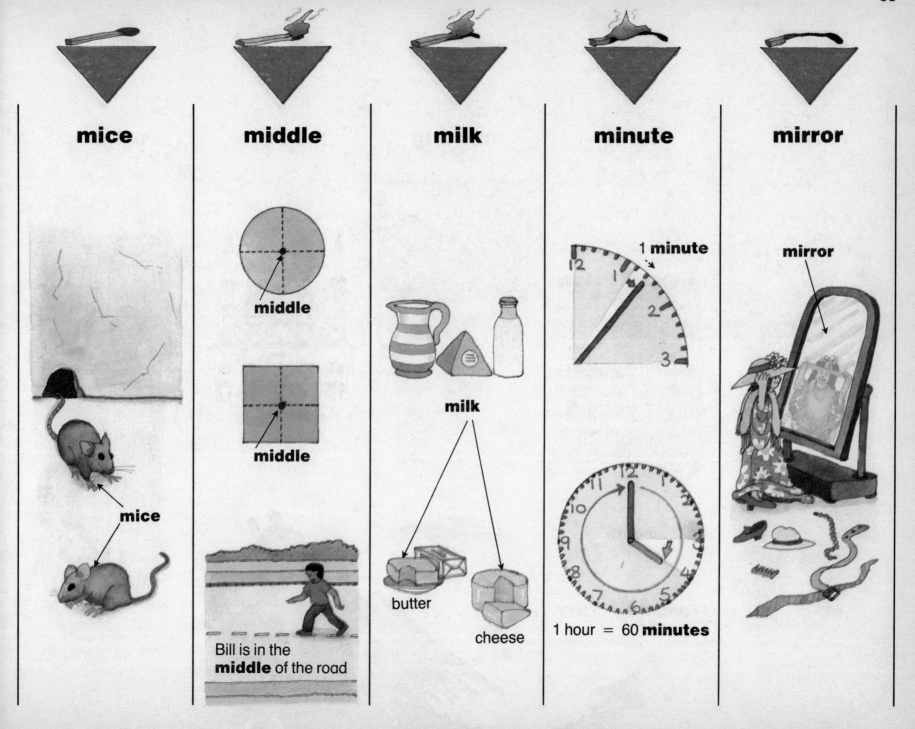

mice

middle

milk

minute

mirror

middle

middle

Bill is in the **middle** of the road

milk

butter

cheese

1 **minute**

1 hour = 60 **minutes**

mirror

mice

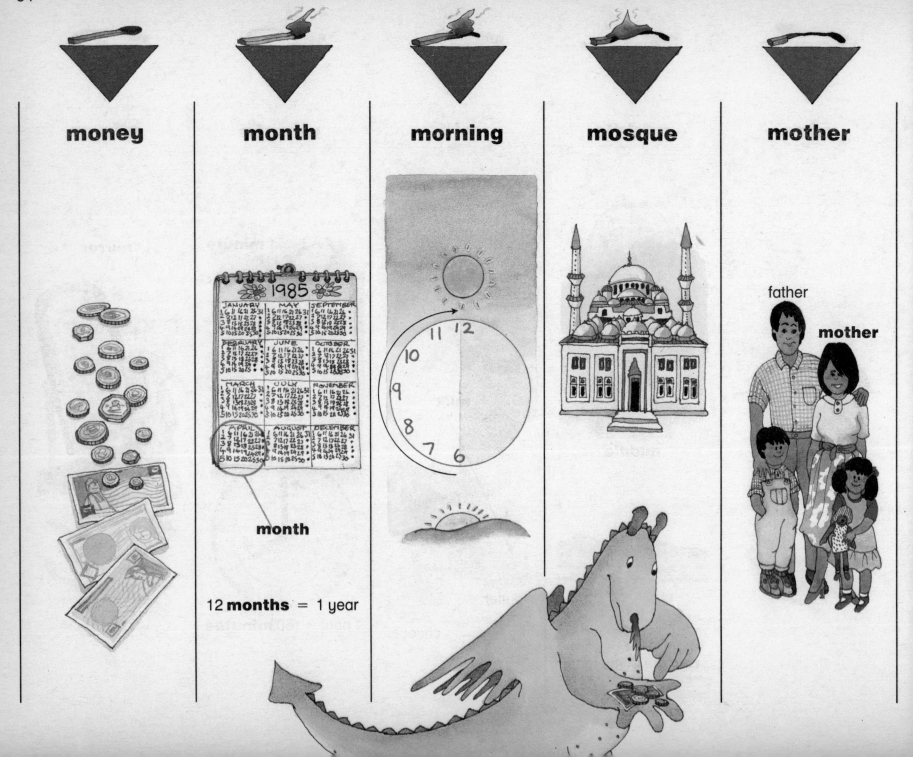

money

month

morning

mosque

mother

1985

month

12 **months** = 1 year

father

mother

motorbike

mountain

mouse

mouth

multiply

mountain

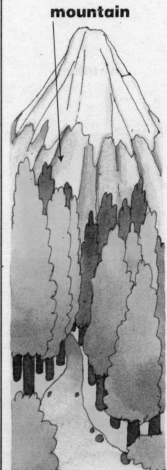

mouse

mouth

divide 10 by 2

multiply 10 by 2

multiply = ×

nail

neck
necklace

needle

newspaper

nail

neck

necklace

needle

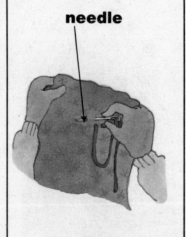

nine
nineteen
ninety

nine = 9

nineteen = 19

ninety = 90

nose

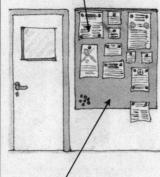

nose

notice
noticeboard

notice

noticeboard

now

Bob Smith — **now**

Bob Smith —
50 years ago

Bob Smith—
70 years ago

nurse

nurse

O o

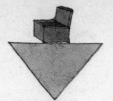

o'clock

2 **o'clock**

2 **o'clock**

on

on the table

under the table

over

under

one

1

one = 1

2

two = 2

3

three = 3

onion

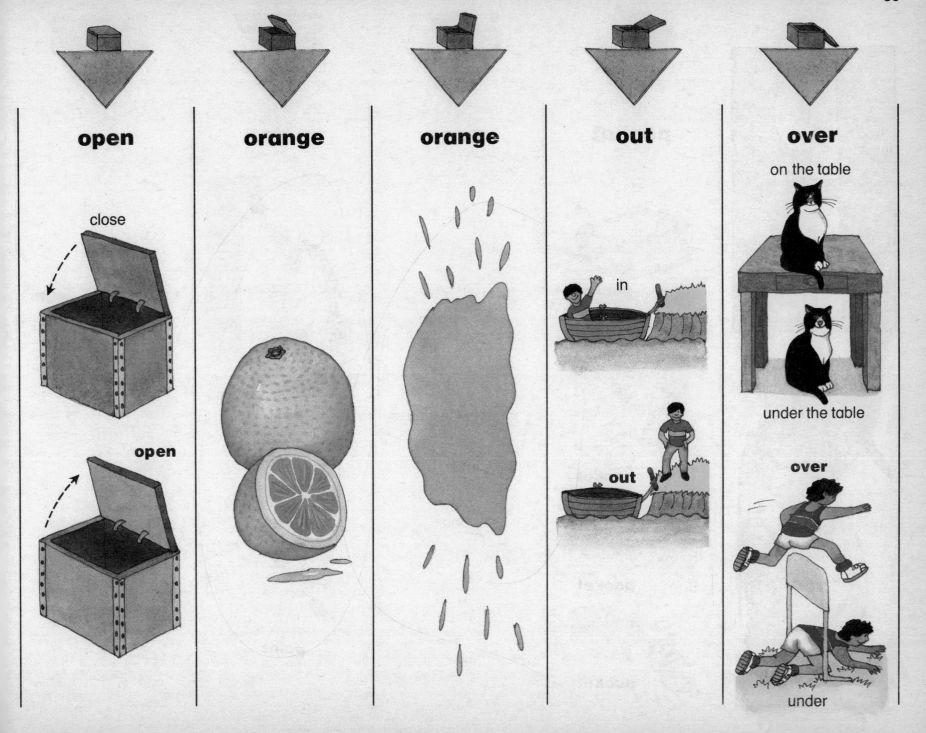

open

orange

orange

out

over

close

open

on the table

under the table

in

out

over

under

60

  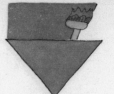 

packet

packet

packet

packet

packet

page

page

book

paint

paint

paint

pan

pan

pan

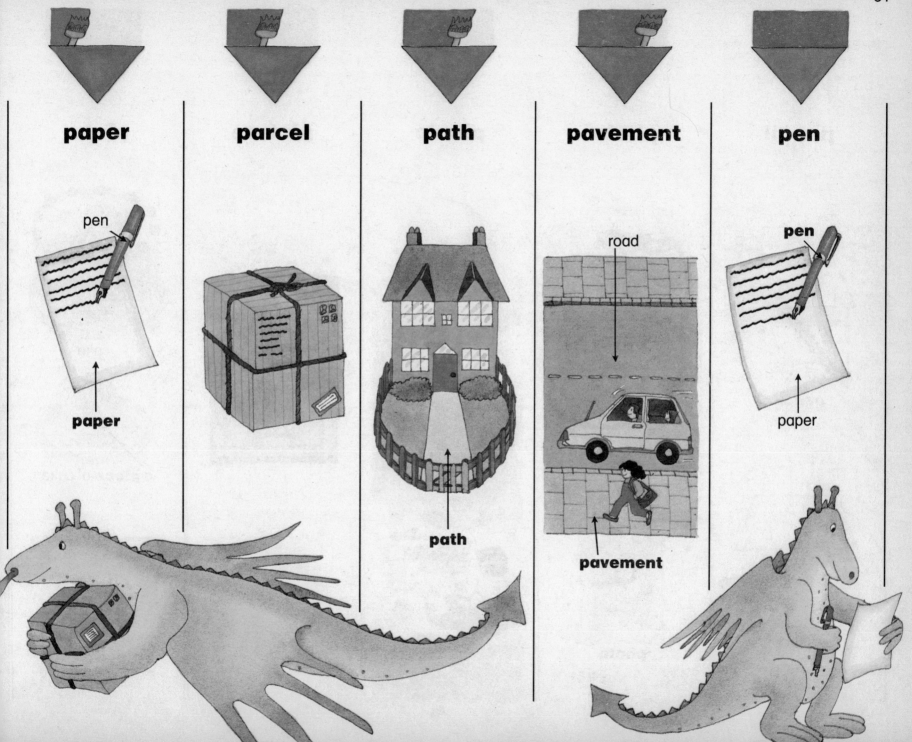

paper

parcel

path

pavement

pen

pen

paper

road

pavement

pen

paper

path

62

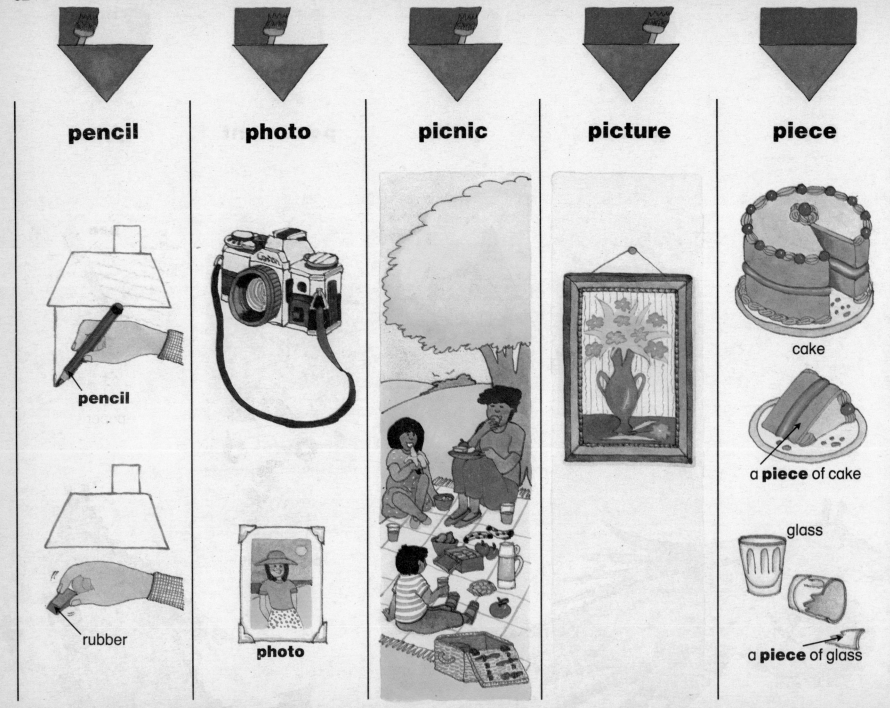

pencil

pencil

rubber

photo

photo

picnic

picture

piece

cake

a **piece** of cake

glass

a **piece** of glass

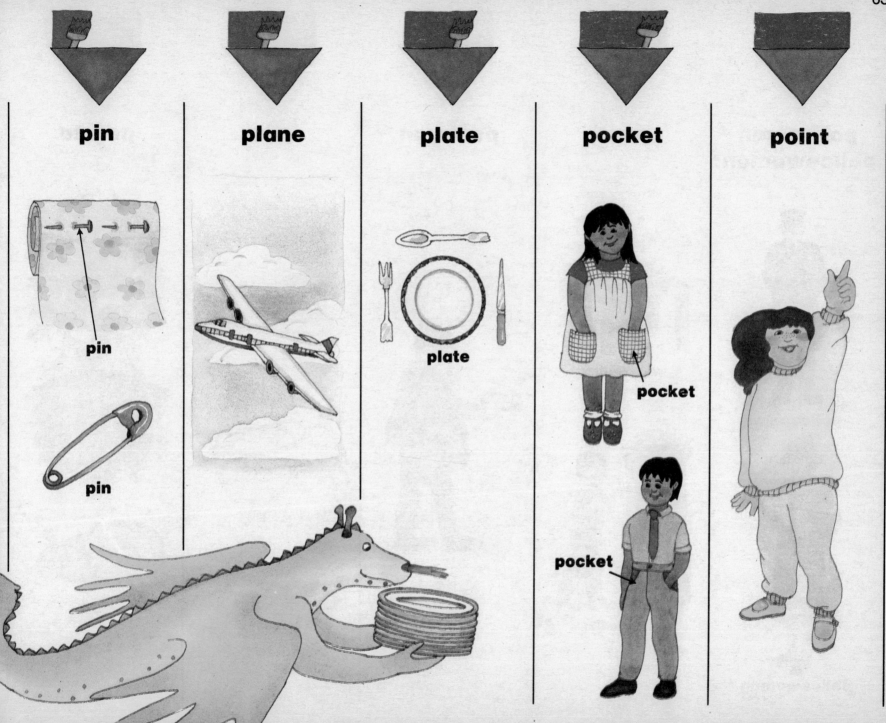

pin

plane

plate

pocket

point

pin

pin

plate

pocket

pocket

policeman
policewoman

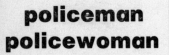

post

postman

pot

potato

policeman

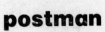

write a letter

pot

policewoman

post a letter

pot

pot

pull   **pupil**   **puppy**   **purse**   **push**

pupil   teacher

dog

<--- **pull**

<---- pull

<--- push

class

puppy

purse

purse

<--- **push**

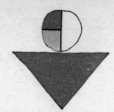

quarter

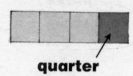

quarter

quarter

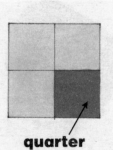

quarter

quarter = ¼

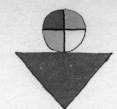

quarter to

four o'clock

quarter to four

quarter to four
= 3.45

3:45

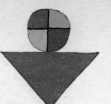

quarter past

four o'clock

quarter past four

quarter past four
= 4.15

4:15

queen

king

queen

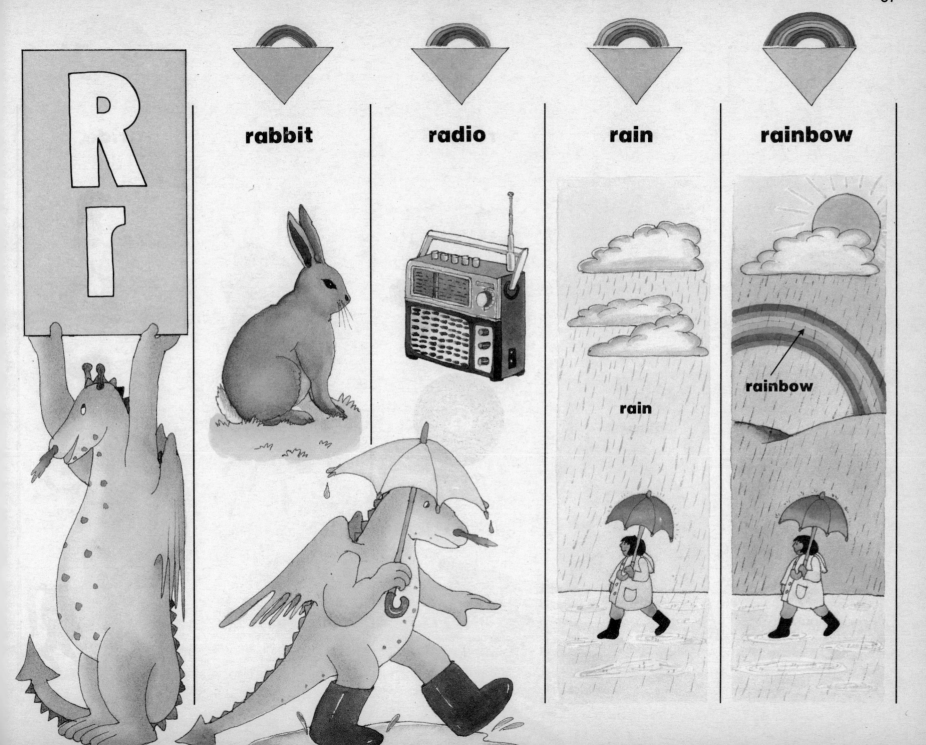

67

R **r**

rabbit

radio

rain

rainbow

rain

rainbow

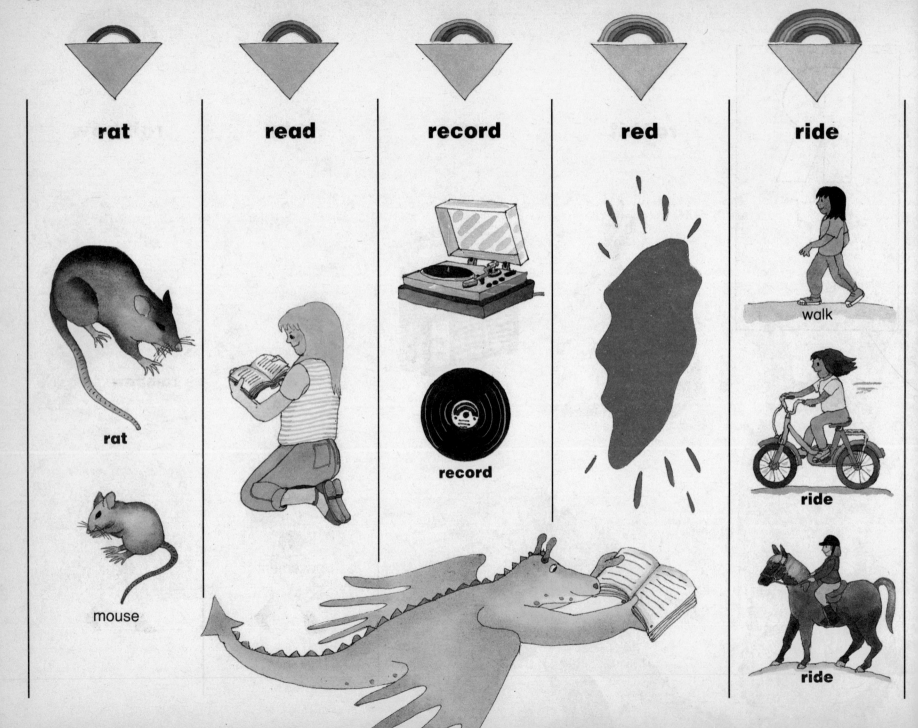

rat

rat

mouse

read

record

record

red

ride

walk

ride

ride

right

right

river

road

roof

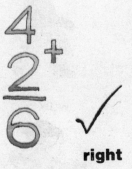
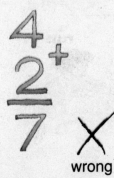

4 2 6 + ✓ **right**

4 2 7 + ✗ wrong

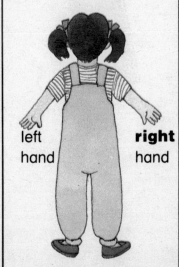

right hand   left hand

left hand   **right** hand

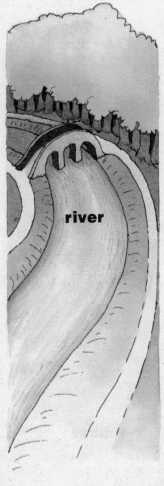

river

road

pavement

roof

wall   window

room	round	rubber	ruler	run

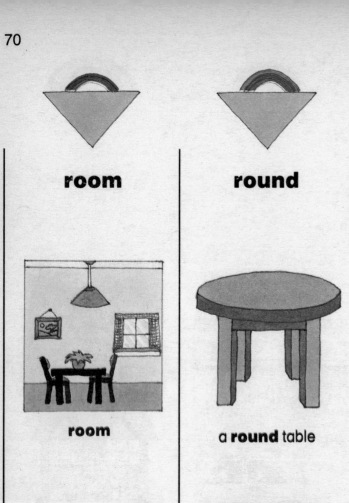

room

room

room

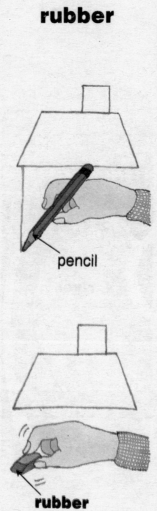

a **round** table

a square table

pencil

rubber

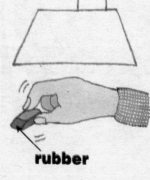

walk

run

jump

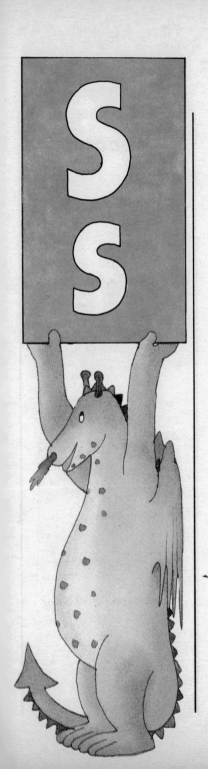

S

sad   **sand**   **sandal**   **sandwich**

Jim is happy

sand

sandal

sandwich

Jim is **sad**

sand

shoe

sandwich

sandwich

71

 **saucer**

 **scissors**

sea

 **seat**

second

saucer

sea

beach

seat

seat

seat

seat

second   first   third

second / 2nd May

| **see** | **seven**
 seventeen
 seventy | **sew** | **sheep** | **ship** |

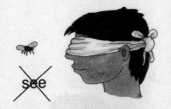

see

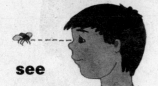

look

seven = 7

seventeen = 17

seventy = 70

sew

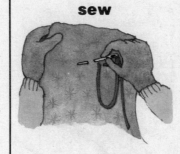

sew

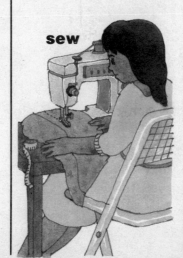

lamb

sheep

74

shirt

shirt

shoe

sandal

shoe

shop

shop

shop

shop

short

short hair

long hair

Tom is tall

Sam is **short**

shoulder

shoulder

shout

shut

side

sing

sit

talk

shout

shut

open

front

back

side

sing

sing

stand

sit

kneel

six
sixteen
sixty

skirt

sky

sleep

slow

six = 6

sixteen = 16

sixty = 60

skirt

sky

sea

walk

eat

sleep

1 km in 5 hours
= **slow**

1 km in 5 minutes
= fast

small

smile

smoke

snow

soap

a big dog

a **small** dog

smile

laugh

smoke

snow

soap

sock

soldier

some

son

spoon

Some leaves are on the ground

All the leaves are on the ground

son

daughter

spoon

fork

knife

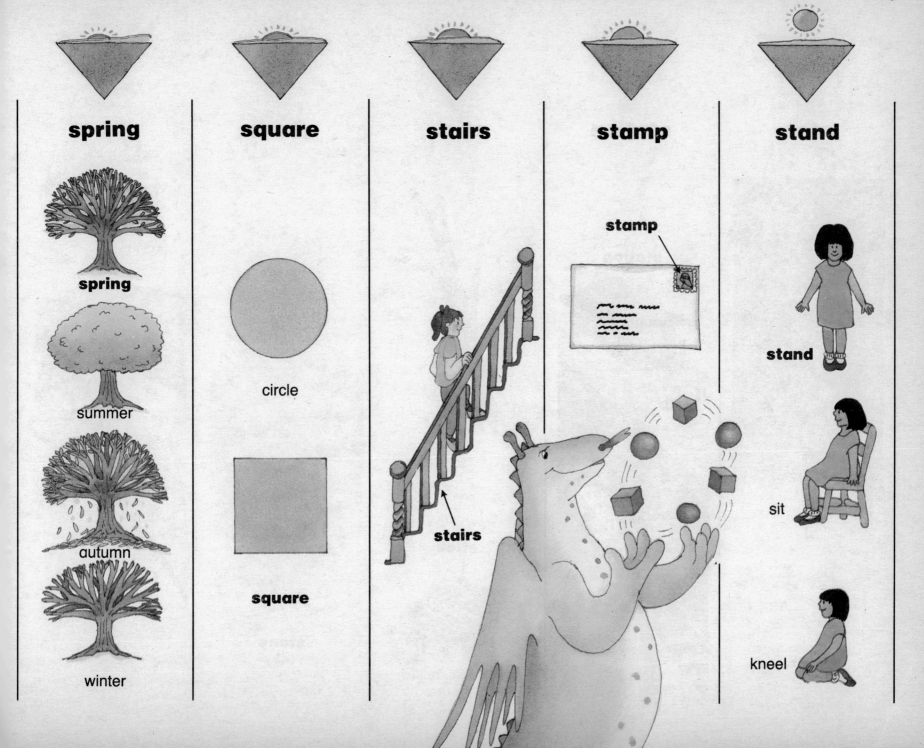

spring

spring

summer

autumn

winter

square

circle

square

stairs

stairs

stamp

stamp

stand

stand

sit

kneel

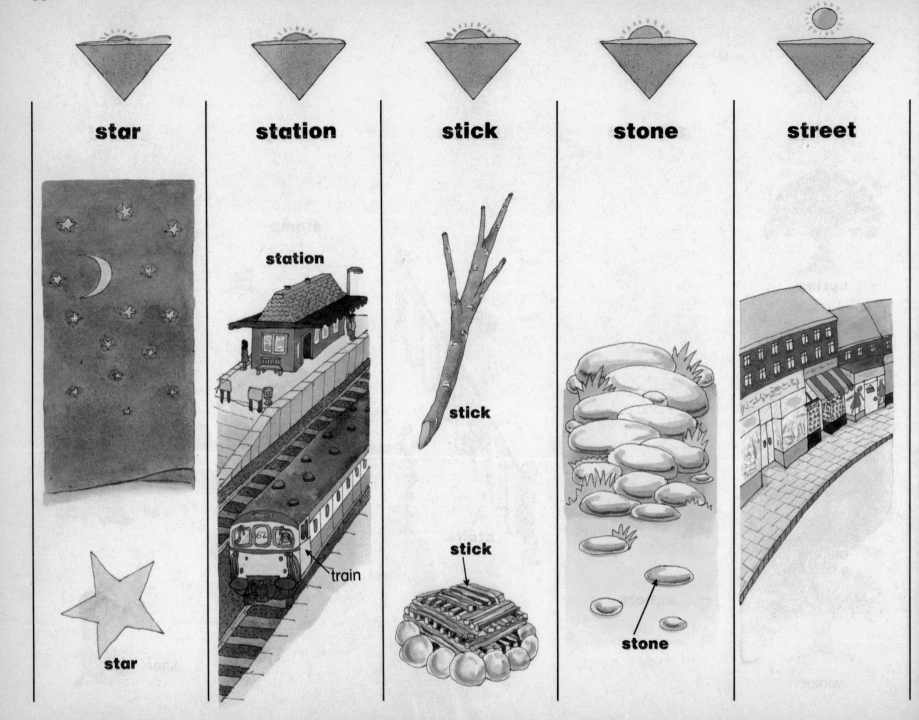

star   **station**   **stick**   **stone**   **street**

station

star

train

stick

stick

stone

stone

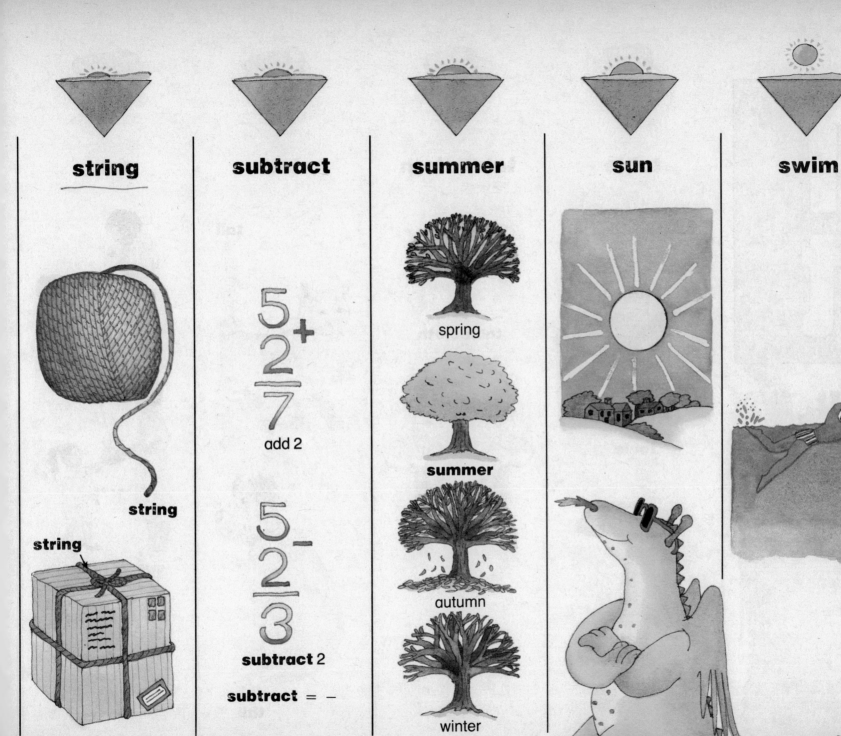

string

subtract

summer

sun

swim

string

string

$$\frac{\begin{array}{r}5\\2+\end{array}}{7}$$
add 2

$$\frac{\begin{array}{r}5\\2-\end{array}}{3}$$
subtract 2

subtract = −

spring

summer

autumn

winter

T t

table

table

table

tablecloth

tablecloth

tail

tail

tail

take

give   take

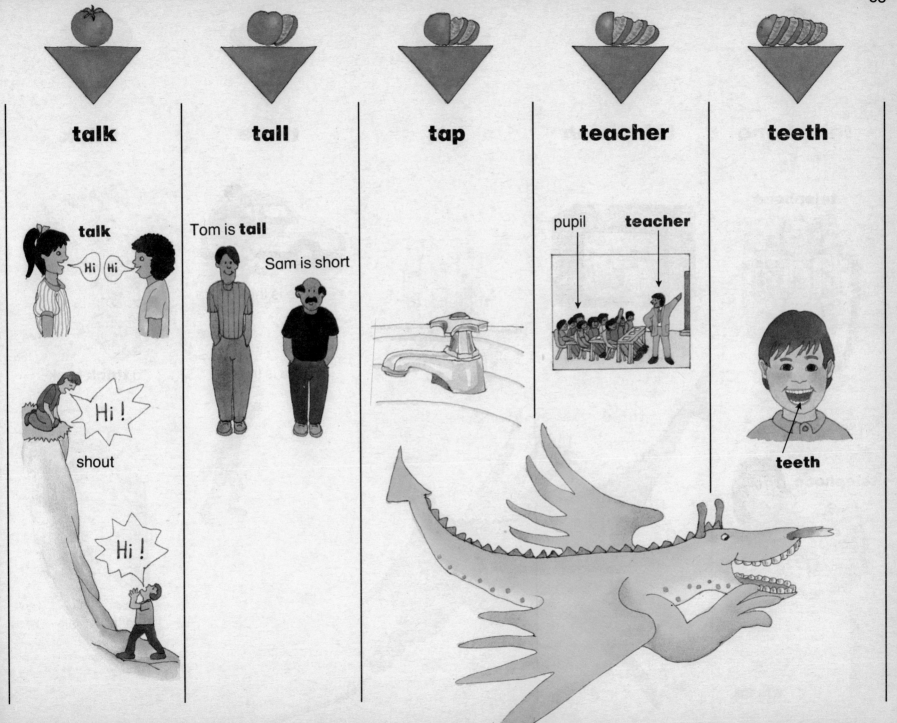

talk

tall

tap

teacher

teeth

talk

Hi Hi

Hi !

shout

Hi !

Tom is **tall**

Sam is short

pupil **teacher**

teeth

telephone

television

ten

there

thick

telephone

ten = 10

Here is the car

There is the car

a **thick** book

a thin book

telephone

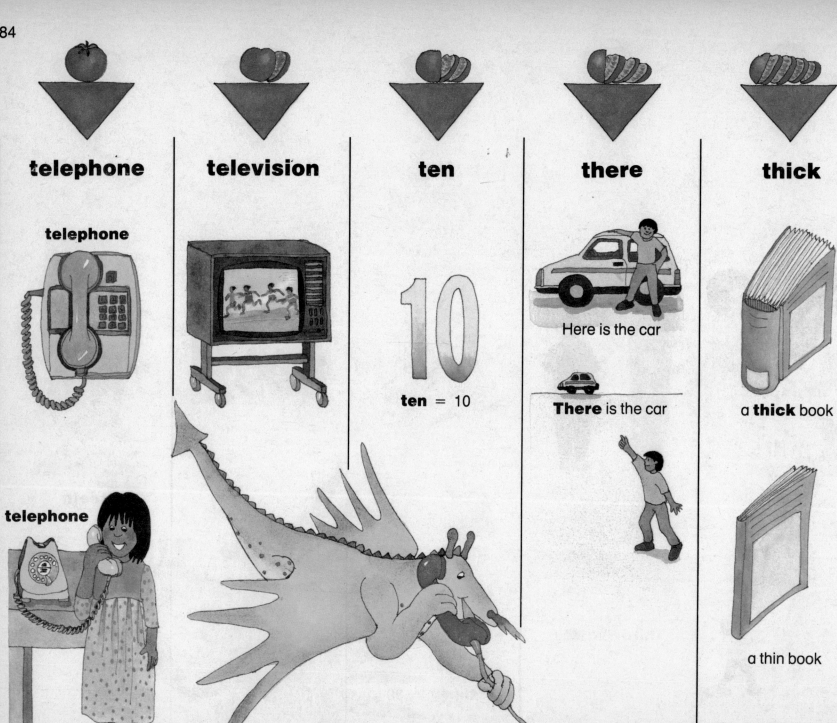

thin

third

three
thirteen
thirty

throw

thumb

a thick book

a **thin** book

Fred is fat

Tim is **thin**

second **first** **third**

third / 3rd May

three = 3

thirteen = 13

thirty = 30

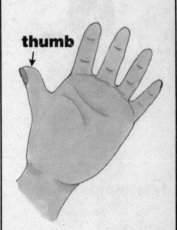

throw

catch

thumb

tie

tin

toe

tomato

tongue

tie

tin

toe

tongue

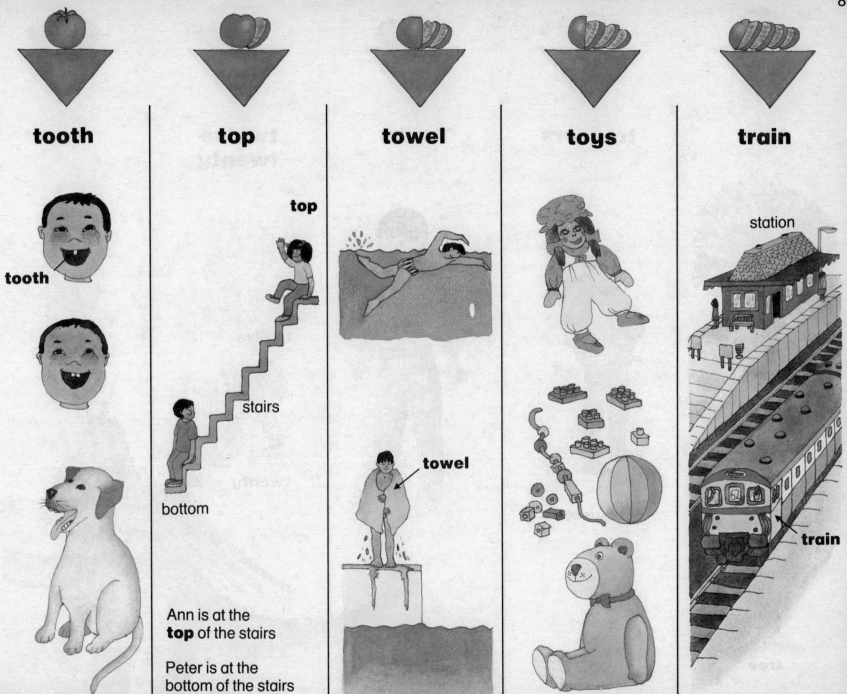

tooth

tooth

top

top

stairs

bottom

Ann is at the
top of the stairs

Peter is at the
bottom of the stairs

towel

towel

toys

train

station

train

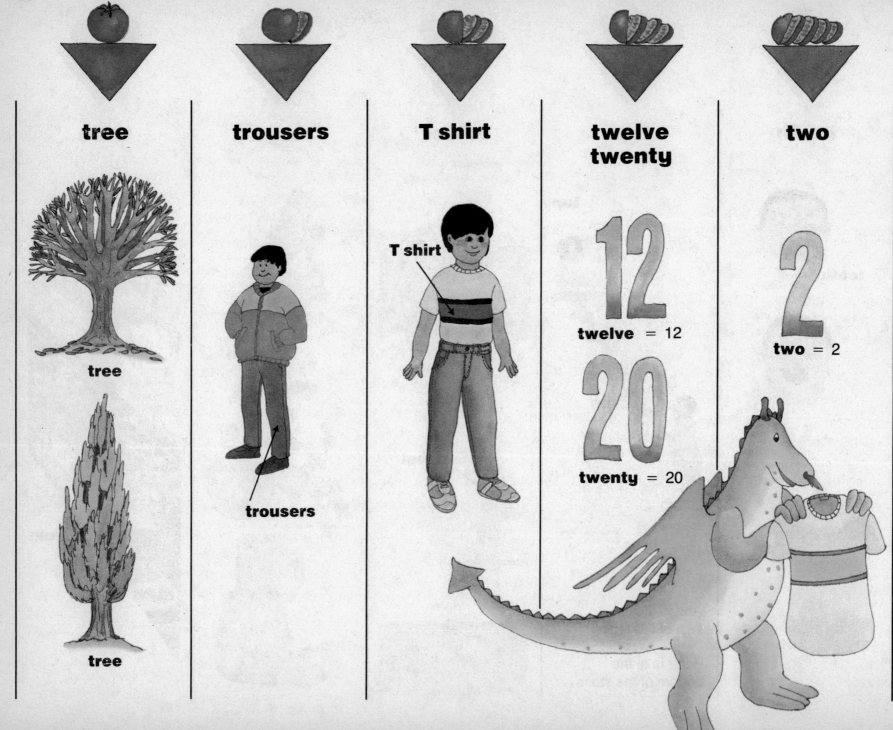

tree

tree

tree

trousers

trousers

T shirt

T shirt

twelve
twenty

twelve = 12

twenty = 20

two

two = 2

U u

umbrella

umbrella

under

on the table

under the table

over

under

unhappy

Jim is happy

Jim is **unhappy**

up

down

up

90

V v

valley

van

lorry

van

vegetables

very

short

long

very long

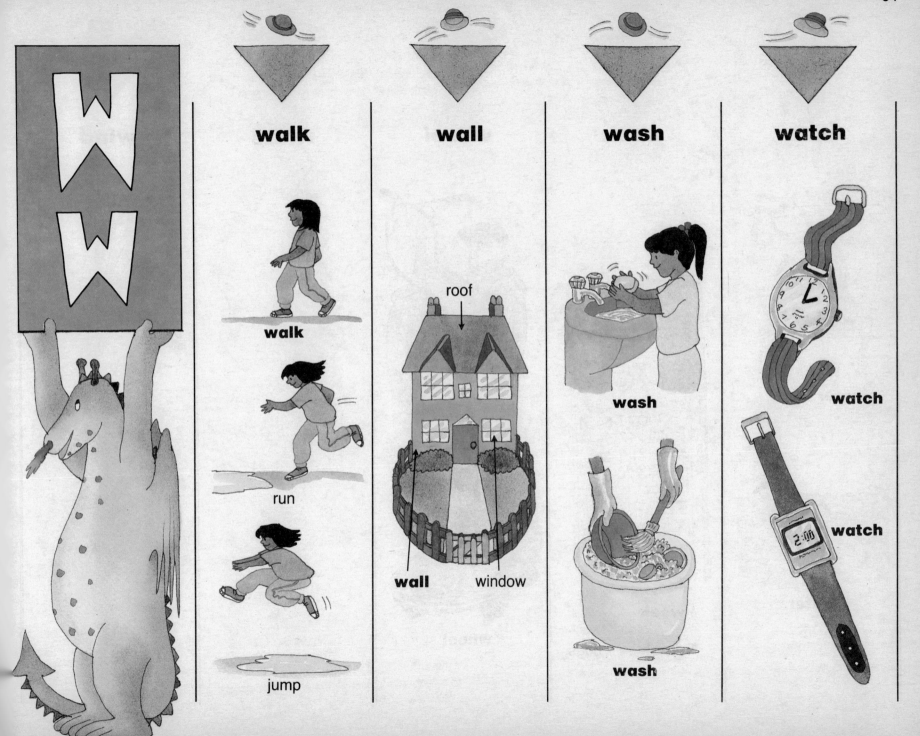

W

walk

walk

run

jump

wall

roof

wall window

wash

wash

wash

watch

watch

watch

| **water** | **week** | **wheel** | **white** | **wind** |

water

water

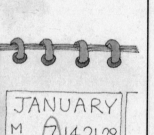

JANUARY

M 7 14 21 28
T 1 8 15 22 29
W 2 9 16 23 30
Th 3 10 17 24 31
F 4 11 18 25
S 5 12 19 26
Sn 6 13 20 27

FEBRUARY

M 4 11 18 25
T 5 12 19 26
W 6 13 20 27

1 week

1 week = 7 days

wheel

wheel

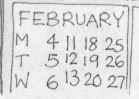

window

winter

woman

write

wrong

roof

wall · **window**

spring

summer

autumn

winter

man

woman

write

write

$\begin{array}{r}4\\2+\\\hline 6\end{array}$ ✓ right

$\begin{array}{r}4\\2+\\\hline 7\end{array}$ ✗ **wrong**

XYZ
xyz

X-ray

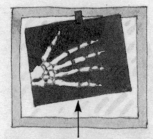

X-ray

year

1 **year** = 12 months

yellow

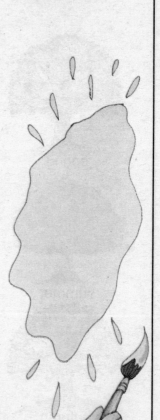

zip

zip

zip

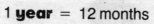